WHIPS AND CHAINS

A BILLIONAIRE & A VIRGIN ROMANCE

CELESTE FALL

HOT AND STEAMY ROMANCE

CONTENTS

Synopsis	v
1. Chapter One	1
2. Chapter Two	5
3. Chapter Three	9
4. Chapter Four	15
5. Chapter Five	19
6. Chapter Six	24
7. Chapter Seven	29
8. Chapter Eight	35
9. Chapter Nine	47
10. Chapter Ten	52
11. Chapter Eleven	55
12. Chapter Twelve	57
Sign Up to Receive Free Books	65
Preview of First Love	66
Chapter One	68
Chapter Two	72
Chapter Three	75
Chapter Four	77
Chapter Five	81
Chapter Six	85
Other Books By This Author	89
Copyright	91

Made in "The United States" by:

Celeste Fall

© Copyright 2020 – Celeste Fall

ISBN: 978-1-64808-057-9

ALL RIGHTS RESERVED. No part of this publication may be reproduced or transmitted in any form whatsoever, electronic, or mechanical, including photocopying, recording, or by any informational storage or retrieval system without express written, dated and signed permission from the author

❦ Created with Vellum

SYNOPSIS

As a teenager, growing up dirt-poor, beautiful, brainy Tracie Rutherford knew education was her ticket out of this Skunk's Hollow cycle of poverty. Consequently, she developed a reputation as an "ice maiden." But her hard work paid off in the shape of a full scholarship to the University of Georgia. Meeting handsome, charismatic billionaire Jamie Spelling seemed like a dream come true. Still a virgin, Tracie's first sexual experience with her seasoned lover was mind-blowing. Jamie's mother's disapproval of this "trollop" who had forced her way into their family was palpable. She was simply "not their kind." But Tracie's honest, eager attitude won the hearts of Jamie's grandmother, Audra Spelling, and her companion, bold, brassy billionaire rancher, Lottie Chambers. When Jamie's sexual fantasies and his demands made Tracie realize she was merely a commodity to please her husband's rich clients, she sought the help of these two women who helped her realize her potential.

When University of Georgia freshman Jamie Spellman spies strikingly beautiful economics classmate Tracie Rutherford, it was lust at first sight. Unaccustomed to being denied anything—

or anyone—he wants, Jamie is shocked and fascinated to discover the beautiful, blonde, brainy girl is still a virgin. A whirlwind romance culminates in Jamie's taking Tracie for his bride. His billionaire parents are unimpressed as his mother has already selected a wealthy girl with the proper pedigree for her only son. Follow the downward spiral of this increasingly depraved relationship to discover if love conquers all.

"I will not spend my life in poverty and pregnancy in Skunk's Hollow!" teenage Tracie Rutherford promises herself. She dreams of a life where money and success are possible. When she meets darkly handsome billionaire Jamie Spellman, it seems like her fairy-tale dream is at last coming true. Still a virgin, the brainy economics student is swept off her feet by Jamie's wining and dining and sexual antics. Little does Tracie know the price she will pay for success. Follow Tracie's adventure as her life takes strange turns

1
CHAPTER ONE

Not in My Backyard

Thirty-one-year-old Tracie Spellman pushed her artfully streaked blonde hair out of her eyes and reached blindly for the Snooze button on her annoyingly persistent alarm clock. Her head throbbed. Her body ached. It even hurt to open and close her eyes.

With a groan, she rolled over. That's when she noticed the blood-streaked sheets and the stickiness between her legs.

What the hell happened last night?

While she was trying to collect her senses and her recollections, a sharp knock sounded at the door. Tracie squinted at the clock. Her head pounded.

8:04

Christ! Who'd be bothering her at this hour?

The door opened and in whisked her secretary, Avril Steele. Her Prada shoes clicked purposefully on the shiny oak floor as she bustled briskly across the spacious room to Tracie's bedside. She fixed her steely gray eyes on Tracie's disheveled appearance and sniffed in distain. Tracie was pretty sure her prim British assistant could smell sex in the air around her.

"What do you want, Avril?" Tracie groaned. She knew her assistant's presence at this hour couldn't be a good sign.

"Madame," Avril began, glancing pointedly at her watch, "when Master Jamie left for work over an hour ago, he asked me to wake you and remind you of your meeting with Mrs. Chambers at nine."

"Oh, no! Is that today?" The pounding in her head increased to jackhammer intensity.

"Well, this is July 8, so, yes, the meeting is today," Avril replied patiently, as if she were talking to a three-year-old.

Tracie hated Avril's condescending attitude. The efficient, yet irritating, forty-year-old had not been Tracie's choice. She hadn't wanted an assistant at all. But if she was forced to hire one, she wanted someone who was younger and more fun. But Jamie, as always, had the last word. He insisted that his attractive wife needed someone who would "keep her on track" and "establish a routine" in Tracie's life. In other words, someone to whom Tracie would be accountable when Jamie was at work.

When Tracie and Jamie had met at college and fallen in love, the poor girl from the wrong side of the tracks in her small southern Alabama town of Skunk's Hollow had had no idea how wide a gap separated their lives.

Tracie was in for her first rude awakening when Jamie brought her home to his massive Montgomery estate. Her mind traveled back while Avril strode to her closet to select an appropriate outfit for her meeting.

With a quiet groan, Tracie gathered the soiled sheets around her and headed for the shower. She had no energy for sparring with meddlesome Lottie Chambers today.

Why does Jamie get her involved in these touchy issues? she wondered. *Or, is this the work of his mother?*

When she'd met the intimidating Marilyn Spellman, it had been hate at first sight. The dark-haired, statuesque matriarch had left nothing to the imagination. She loathed Tracie's mere existence.

And as for this little gold digger ever being part of my family? Never! Charity might begin at home, but not in my son's bedroom! according to Marilyn.

All efforts on Jamie's part to negotiate a truce between the two women he loved most fell on unresponsive ears. Marilyn Spellman might be the undisputed champion of fundraisers for local food banks and homeless shelters. But when it came to her family? She didn't care a fig about how Tracie had pulled herself out of the slums and graduated top of her class at Emory. She would never be welcome under Marilyn's roof. All Jamie's eloquent pleading to his mother to put herself in Tracie's shoes had no effect on Marilyn. Her mind was made up. This girl was bad news, and the sooner Jamie came to his senses and dumped her, the better!

To be fair, Tracie admitted, she and Jamie's mother did not get off on the right foot when Marilyn burst into Jamie's bedroom and found Tracie on her knees in front of Jamie, performing fellatio. Two nights in widely separated bedrooms had taken their toll on the pair accustomed to sleeping together at Emory. They were merely getting reacquainted and letting off some pent-up sexual steam.

Marilyn didn't see it that way. She was convinced Tracie was a low-life, promiscuous woman who would fall upon whatever was put in front of her. The Spellman wealth was not going to become this girl's opportunity, if Marilyn had anything to say about it. She had pretty socialite Tiffany King in her sights, as soon as she could make her son see things sensibly. Tiffany would be a fine match. She was their kind of people!

So the two women gave each other a wide berth. Jamie never

took Tracie home again, until she was wearing his grandmother's diamond engagement ring. There was nothing Marilyn Spellman could do except pitch a fit. The three-carat diamond belonged to Jamie's paternal grandmother, Audra Spellman, who adored Tracie and was thrilled to pass on the family heirloom to her only grandson and his bride-to-be. Marilyn did a slow burn and waited for the right moment to rid the family of this white trash.

Audra also insisted upon hosting and paying for the wedding. Tracie was torn. She hadn't been home or talked to her parents since she graduated from high school. She wanted them to know she was doing well, but she didn't want to rub their noses in her success. Although they could make the trip to Audra's mansion in Montgomery, it was unlikely that they'd even consider it. They wouldn't know how to dress, how to act, or how to talk to these people. Meeting her parents would give Marilyn Spellman further fuel to highlight the gap between Jamie and Tracie. The Spellmans and the Rutherfords were as different as two sides of a coin, as sharply contrasting as black and white, as likely to hit it off as fire and gas. It was a disaster waiting to happen! Tracie had worked so hard to rid herself of the stench of Skunk's Hollow. She was reluctant to bring the two disparate sides of her life together. She'd moved on and worked hard to make a new life for herself.

2

CHAPTER TWO

Avril's Dilemma

As she gathered the ripped, soiled sheet around her and headed to the bathroom, Tracie could hear Avril's muttering in the cavernous walk-in closet where she was selecting the "least inappropriate" outfit for Tracie to wear to this important meeting with Lottie Chambers. She paused for a moment, wondering if she should shoo Avril out of her closet. Then, with a shrug and an evil little smile, she continued on her way to the bathroom. "Let the old bat think whatever she wants," Tracie muttered.

AVRIL SAW her job as a daily battle of wills to try to mold the reluctant Tracie into the family representative. Marilyn and Alan Spellman would have wanted for their son and her to be part of Spellman Investments. She'd been at it ever since Tracie had become Jamie's bride at age twenty-eight. But, so far, it was a losing battle. The Spellmans had offered Avril handsome financial incentives for whipping their daughter-in-law into shape. In a battle of wills, Avril was usually up for the challenge. But, it seemed that she'd met her match. Tracie wasn't like the other pampered, spoiled little rich girls whom Avril had been sent to dispatch after Master Jamie had awakened to find the inconvenient conquest resting her head on his shoulder. Tracie was a tough nut with street smarts. Clearly, she had no notion of being spirited away by the intimidating Avril. This girl had substance. Avril was grudgingly appreciative of her backbone—if not her manners or her deplorable taste in clothing.

True, the Spellmans had won a battle when Avril was chosen as the new Mrs. Spellman's secretary. There was no doubt that she'd never have been Tracie's choice. Avril knew she wasn't young enough or hip enough or fun enough to suit Tracie. The young blonde acted like a teenager. She had no idea what her role should be—nor did she seem to care. And as for Master Jamie? He was so smitten—fuckstruck, Avril thought to herself—that he couldn't see how his wife's attitude was hurting his reputation and that of the company. Spellman Financial could not afford a false step. Avril had heard Jamie and his father discussing some bad investments and their need to woo new clients and offer incentives to their present clients to stay. She knew that, if the company hoped to stay afloat, the Spellmans had to do some fancy manipulating. Frankly, Avril did not see the new Mrs. Spellman as an asset in that department.

However, Avril knew how important it was for Tracie to make a good impression on Lottie Chambers. Tracie seemed unaware or unconcerned about how much was riding on this meeting. Avril shook her head in dismay as she scrutinized Tracie's wardrobe. Nothing here spoke of business and good breeding. At best, the clothes were frivolous. And at worst, they were simply poorly designed and bad fashion sense.

As she worked her way down the rows of clothing arranged in no particular order, Avril made a note to return to the closet and establish some order with the maid who picked up after Tracie dropped her clothes anywhere. She had just about come to the end of the massive closet when her hand hit a leather garment in the dark corner. When she pulled it off the rod, she gasped in horror. Hanging from a padded hanger was a black leather bustier. In a box below it, she discovered thigh-high black leather boots and a whip with braided lashes that ended in metal studs. What appeared to be blood coated several of the studs.

Avril pulled back her hand as if she'd been burned. *What on earth is this girl playing at?*

Unable to resist, Avril plunged her hand farther into the box. The next item she pulled out was a set of fur-lined handcuffs. There were a handful of silk scarves in various stages of wrinkle and knot. Out came a giant purple feather. Then, in the very bottom of the box, Avril extracted a pair of shiny black leather gloves. Examining them closely, she noted a greasy substance, which looked suspiciously like Vaseline, coated the palms and fingers. Avril shuddered and swallowed deep breaths to keep from being sick.

What on earth were these two up to? she wondered. She recalled the blood-stained sheet, which appeared to have slits cut into its Egyptian cotton threads. Images rose unbidden to her troubled mind.

Should I report this to the Spellmans? Should I mention it to Master Jamie? Was he part of this, or were the things I found part of Tracie's sordid past?

AVRIL DECIDED to do nothing until she knew more about what was going on. This might have been a costume for a masquerade. Rich people had strange diversions. She quickly snapped photos of the garments and the other paraphernalia with her phone.

THEN, with a sigh, she chose the least objectionable of Tracie's outfits and left it on a chair by the bathroom door.

3
CHAPTER THREE

Like a Virgin

Hot water flowed over Tracie's aching body. With a soft washcloth, she probed the depths of her core, wincing as her sweet spot proved to be anything else but sweet. As she lathered her body and hair with the rich lavender products she liked, she tried to recreate the events of the night before.

SHE RECALLED a loud party and far too much champagne. She remembered someone—it might have been Jamie—feeding her toast points piled high with beluga caviar. She knew she'd washed it down with the finest vodka money could buy.

SHE HAD no idea how she'd gotten to bed or who had undressed her.

. . .

Where are my clothes? Did I hang them up?

She had a foggy idea of whips and chains and four-inch high heels on hip-high boots with spurs.

Did I dream all this? If so, why are the sheets blood smeared? Had the sex been that rough? She didn't think so. Sure, she was sore. But there were no lacerations.

Then, who bled on the sheets?

With a contented smile, Tracie recalled her first meeting with Jamie. She was majoring in political science, and Jamie was getting a business degree. Their programs both required introductory economics and statistics. Tracie noticed the handsome, auburn-haired hunk with the surfer's body. He'd glanced at her, his startling green eyes sweeping over her. After their first economics seminar, he'd introduced himself and invited her for coffee. They'd talked about everything: new movies, music they enjoyed, books they'd read. They laughed over classmates' bizarre behavior. Jamie had her in stitches when he mimicked their professors.

When Jamie walked her back to her dorm, he'd leaned in and placed a butterfly-light kiss on her forehead. "See you tomorrow, Tracie Rutherford," he'd called back over his shoulder.

The next day, he'd called to ask her to work on a statistics assignment together. Tracie was so smitten with the gorgeous, popular boy with the killer smile that she could scarcely wait to get to class each day.

THERE FOLLOWED A WHIRLWIND ROMANCE. In the city no longer than she had been, Jamie seemed to know the *in* places. They ate in some amazing Atlanta restaurants, attended sporting events, concerts, and theater.

THEY WENT for long drives in the BMW coup his parents had given him for graduation and engaged in some heavy petting that steamed up the windows of the baby blue automobile. "Your first time is going to be memorable," Jamie told her one night when they both withdrew, panting with longing.

"How—how did you know I'm a virgin?" she asked. "Oh, no! I'm a complete novice, aren't I?"

"NO!" Jamie assured her. "You give head very enthusiastically."

"THEN I KISS LIKE A SIX-YEAR-OLD!" Tracie wailed.

"OF COURSE NOT!" Jamie assured her, planting kisses on her nose, her chin, and her forehead. "Your kisses send me to take cold showers."

"THEN WHAT GAVE ME AWAY?" she asked sadly.

. . .

"Promise you won't get mad?" Jamie demanded.

"Just tell me," Tracie snapped.

"Well," Jamie continued, "I've never met a girl who creamed her pants just sitting beside me. It's very flattering. I promise, your first time will be mind-blowing."

Jamie had been as good as his word. They'd dined at an expensive Atlanta steakhouse complete with flowers at the table, a violinist to serenade them, and champagne.

The champagne had made Tracie sneeze. She was giddy after the second glass.

Then they'd walked up the street, arms around one another, to a posh hotel where Jamie had reserved the bridal suite. They'd feasted on chocolate-covered strawberries and more champagne as they soaked in the heart-shaped hot tub. Then, they'd taken a shower in the enormous walk-in shower stall, where they'd lathered each other with eucalyptus shower gel. Jamie explored every crevice of her body and dried every inch of her throbbing body with a fluffy white towel.

Then, in spite of her pleading, Jamie had patiently and thoroughly caressed, kissed, and suckled every part of her body. When she was a squealing mass of hormones, Jamie began what could only be called cock teasing, inserting his throbbing member into Tracie an inch and then pulling out. This went on for what seemed like hours as Tracie clutched and raked his back and thrust herself at him. The final thrust was such a relief that Tracie scarcely noticed the pain or the bleeding.

THEIR LOVEMAKING EXTENDED WELL into the night. Tracie just couldn't get enough of this heady new experience, and Jamie, in his sexual prime, was literally up for the task.

AFTERWARD, Jamie gently sponged her throbbing crotch and covered her with a sheet. He planted gentle kisses on her face and whispered, "Good night, princess."

WHEN TRACIE AWOKE the next morning, Jamie had breakfast waiting. She quickly brushed her teeth, took a quick shower, and surveyed herself in the mirror. Her skin glowed and she could not wipe the smile off her face.

WRAPPED in fluffy white hotel robes, the two ate a hearty breakfast. Then Jamie asked her what she wanted to do with the day.

"DON'T YOU HAVE A CLASS?" Tracie asked him.

"I AM OFFICIALLY AT YOUR DISPOSAL," Jamie answered.

. . .

"Then I know exactly how I want to spend my day," Tracie announced. "What time do we have to be out of here?"

"Not for hours," Jamie replied. "I just put the Do Not Disturb sign on the door."

"Then, you can proceed any time," Tracie said.

"You're lucky I am at my sexual prime and can meet your needs," Jamie pointed out.

"Yes, I am," Tracie agreed, reaching for him.

CHAPTER FOUR

Whatever It Takes

When people talked about being "swept off their feet" and "love at first sight," practical Tracie Rutherford scoffed outright. For her, there was no poetry and candlelight and violin music. She'd devoted her entire miserable life to escaping the abject poverty of her situation.

Her life had been one struggle after another. The fifth child of seven, she saw what it meant to wear hand-me-downs that had been patched over patches. She knew what it felt like to endure hunger pangs because fried bread was all that was available for breakfast, and her lunch consisted of apples from the tree behind their three-bedroom cabin and leftover breakfast bread—if such a thing existed. Her parents worked from dawn to dusk to scrabble crops from the poor, sandy soil that surrounded their house. By the time they paid the rent on the property, there was precious little to buy flour, sugar, and seeds for the next crop.

As a child, Tracie didn't feel resentful. None of the other kids in the one-room school the Rutherford kids attended had anything either. But Tracie had one thing the others did not have: The strikingly beautiful little girl had a burning desire to escape the poverty in which she'd grown up. As she watched her older sisters and brothers marry and sink into the same hopeless existence her parents lived, she vowed that she'd make something of herself. She'd get out of Skunk's Hollow and never look back.

Besides being beautiful, Tracie Rutherford had smarts. She was book smart and she was street smart. She avoided the boys of Skunk's Hollow and the surrounding communities like the plague. Though they sniffed around her like dogs in heat, Tracie was not about to jeopardize her escape plan by lying with any of them. Sex with those boys could end in only one thing: a life of hard work, starvation, and popping out a kid every year until mercifully, menopause took care of that or her reproductive system just collapsed. She'd seen what happened to her mother and the other neighbor ladies: dull-eyed, toothless creatures who looked twenty years older than their actual age. Tracie was not about to fall into that trap.

So Tracie developed a reputation for being uppity, a cock tease, someone who thought she was better than everybody else. This only intensified the male interest in getting into her pants. Tracie's high school years at nearby Alabaster High were marked by scuffles in the stairwells, where her classmates tried to grope her, and skirmishes behind closed classroom doors, where the randy PE teacher attempted to cop a feel under the guise of helping her explore her sexuality.

Exhausted by fending off these unwanted advances, Tracie sought the help of her guidance counselor, a world-weary sixty-year-old named Amanda Aimes. Her meeting with Miss Aimes was the luckiest thing that happened to the sixteen-year-old. It was no accident that the red-haired, green-eyed woman had chosen guidance. Herself a product of the dirt-farm existence in lower Alabama, Amanda Aimes had used her academic ability to escape the cycle of misery she saw in her community. Having endured the snide comments, sexual assaults, and physical abuse of her family and neighbors, Amanda had been befriended by her high school guidance teacher.

Lydia Percy took Amanda under her wing. She helped her apply for scholarships and assisted her with settling in at Emory, where she got a teaching degree. Although Amanda had vowed never to return to southern Alabama, when the guidance position came up at Alabaster, Amanda took it as a sign that she should "pay it forward." To that end, she had been helping people like Tracie escape their past for thirty years now.

When Tracie secured a full scholarship to the University of Georgia, just outside Atlanta, she was the happiest girl in the world. She loved the fact that this flagship college touting itself as the birthplace of higher education was not in a big city. She vowed she'd make Miss Aimes proud of her. With money given to her by the guidance staff, she bought a one-way bus ticket to Athens, Georgia.

Tracie—who'd hardly ever been outside Alabaster and Skunk's Hollow—fell immediately in love with this university town an hour northeast of Atlanta. With a population of over a hundred thousand, this sixth-largest Georgia city had the feel of a large town. The University of Georgia was literally a town within a town. Tracie also liked the sense of history of the campus.

Its first buildings had actually been made from logs. Lots around the campus were sold in the early 1800s to raise money to build more university buildings. When the first class graduated in 1804, the town of Athens had only three homes, three stores, and a few other buildings on Front Street. This street was later renamed Broad Street. Franklin College, completed in 1806, was the University of Georgia's first permanent structure. This brick building—named in honor of Ben Franklin—was still standing and called Old College. As she walked through the campus grounds, Tracie felt like she belonged here, that she was a part of an American heritage.

She silently blessed Miss Aimes for giving her this opportunity. And she made a pledge that she would do her best to make this precious gift pay off. Tracie studied campus maps eagerly, familiarizing herself with the bookstore, her dorm building, and the buildings where her classes would be held. She took the self-guided campus tour, made a trip to the UGA Visitors' Center, and checked the UGA Master Calendar to see what events were happening on campus each day. She was grateful that Miss Aimes had suggested she arrive a week earlier than registration so she had a feel for her surroundings before the crowds started to descend.

When the first day of classes rolled around, Tracie was armed with textbooks, a tablet, and UGA sweatshirts. As she headed across campus with her UGA backpack slung over her shoulder, she felt like a college student.

"Let the adventure begin," she cried, throwing her arms into the sultry, southern, subtropical air.

She had no idea what adventures awaited her.

CHAPTER FIVE

Cocktails at Eight

Somehow, it had never occurred to Tracie that Jamie's family was wealthy. Sure, they'd bought him a car for graduation. He had money for fine dining, concerts, and sporting events. But he'd explained that his summers were spent working at his dad's company and that's why he had more disposable income than his friends. Otherwise, Jamie dressed and acted like all the other guys at college.

SHE DONNED the boring outfit Avril had left for her to wear to her meeting with Lottie Chambers and finished the last touches on her makeup. In preparation for this important outing, Tracie recalled her first meeting with Jamie's parents.

WHEN HE PULLED up in the driveway of what Tracie could only call a mansion, a valet opened the door of Jamie's blue sports car. There were at least a dozen high-end luxury cars and limousines parked in the huge circular stone driveway.

Tracie's heart dropped. So much for a low-key dinner with his parents, she thought in dismay. What have I gotten myself into?

IN AN INSTANT, Tracie understood why Jamie had taken her shopping for a cocktail dress and matching shoes. "We can slip in this door and get changed first," Jamie announced.

SPEECHLESS, Tracie followed him. "Don't worry," Jamie said, straightening his tie. "They'll love you."

AS THEY DESCENDED THE STAIRS, a statuesque brunette broke away from the group and eyed Tracie's figure-clinging iridescent blue gown with a steely gaze. "You must be Tracie," she said, extending a clawlike manicured hand. "I'm Marilyn Spellman." Without missing a beat, she kissed her son and said, "Jamie, get the girl a drink and introduce her to our friends." Then, she was gone.

"YOU MUST BE the little trollop that's got Marilyn's knickers in a knot," boomed a loud, raspy voice. "I'm Lottie Chambers and I am amused to meet you! Anyone who causes Marilyn's panties to bunch is an instant friend of mine."

TRACIE WATCHED as the large woman, clad in purple suede and matching hand-tooled cowboy boots, grasped Jamie in a bear hug. "Sugar, you've been away from us far too long," she crooned.

"Lottie, you look marvelous," said Jamie. "Are those new boots?" he asked, inspecting Lottie's silver-heeled leather boots with the silver spurs and toe caps.

Lottie did a little boot-scooting boogie, admiring her footwear as she did so. "Finest boots made in New Mexico," she confirmed. "That's where all the rich Texans go."

Lottie is surprisingly light on her feet for such a substantial woman who'd never see seventy again, Tracie thought. But what a strange guest to have been included on the Spellmans' cocktail party guest list. She knew there was an interesting story there. She'd ask Jamie later. Who was she to judge others?

An elegant woman in a couture gown and dazzling jewelry approached. "Now, Lottie," she chided. "Don't be monopolizing the attention of my favorite grandson. Hello, sweet thing," she said, kissing Jamie.

"I'm your only grandson, Grandma," Jamie said, giving the woman a hug, "Tracie, please say hello to my grandmother, Audra Spellman."

"Pleased to meet you, Mrs. Spellman," Tracie said, curtsying.

. . .

"Oh, Jamie," Audra said, "she is a delight." Turning her attention to Tracie, she said, "Call me Audra, dear."

"Your dress is stunning Mrs.—Audra," murmured Tracie.

"And Lottie's boots?" asked Audra with a twinkle in her eye. "What do you think of them?"

"They are truly... astounding," Tracie remarked.

With a delighted laugh, Audra slapped her grandson on the back. "She'll do just fine, son," Audra pronounced. "Just don't let your mother destroy her."

Audra's caution had been accurate. It was hate at first sight, Tracie remembered. There was nothing she could do to please Marilyn Spellman. She wasn't from the right family. She didn't come from money, and she didn't speak correctly or dress appropriately or even play the right games. Tracie had the distinct impression that Marilyn Spellman had Jamie's bride all lined up and that Tracie's presence was inconvenient and unfortunate.

Tracie surveyed herself in the mirror. When did I become a Marilyn Spellman clone? she wondered as she examined her perfect hair, styled at Marilyn's salon, and her prim business suit, created by Marilyn's favorite designer. Even her purse and shoes came from Marilyn's favorite shop.

. . .

IN TRYING to please my husband, have I sold my soul? she mused.

SHE TOOK a quick look at the rose tattoo that peeked timidly from her bra. When she'd admired Jamie's tattooed chest and buttocks, he insisted she needed to consider body art too. She was squeamish about pain, but she'd agreed to get one just to please Jamie.

WHAT ELSE AM I going to have to do to keep my handsome husband? she thought.

SHE WAS SOON to have an answer to that question.

CHAPTER SIX

Easy Rider

A loud roaring noise, like a jet landing, brought Tracie from the back of the house where she was gardening. In their driveway, a huge motorcycle idled with a leather-clad person astride. When the visor of the helmet flipped up, she realized it was Jamie. He looked lethal, cradling that machine between his legs.

"Hop on!" he invited with a flourish.

"Are you kidding?" she asked. "I'm in my gardening clothes. I can't go for a ride looking like this," she said, eyeing her short, ripped denim shorts and her skimpy bikini top.

"I'd be the envy of the neighborhood if you did," he said, wiggling his eyebrows. "I was sort of hoping you'd break out that leather bustier and those thigh-high boots for your first ride on your new machine."

"My machine?" Tracie asked.

"Well, I figured if you ever got tired of the machine between my legs, there'd be another one to take its place."

"I'll go and change into something sensible for risking my

life on the open road," Tracie commented drily. "Whose bike is this anyhow?"

"It's yours," he replied. "If you like it, we'll get a pair of them and tour the country. This isn't just a bike," he added. "It's a Yamaha Star Venture touring bike. It comes with an all-new hybrid steel frame with an aluminum subframe. The 113-cubic-foot air-cooled V-twin engine is tuned with twin counter balancers. It's engineered to provide a smooth, comfortable ride on any road surface."

When Tracie rolled her eyes, Jamie laughed and said, "Okay. It's a guy thing."

"I was just going to say it's a killer red, and I love the backrest behind the second rider."

"So are you ready?" Jamie asked.

"Okay," Tracie said, taking a deep breath. "But don't get your heart set on twin bikes. I think I'd like to tour the country from the safety of the back seat, clutching you for dear life."

"You are such a sweet talker," Jamie said, hugging her. "Now, let's go," he said, giving her behind a playful smack. "Daylight is wasting."

"How do I look?" she asked.

"Not nearly as enticing as you would wearing that bustier. But a lot safer... I guess. Ready for the open road?" Jamie asked when Tracie had reappeared wearing jeans, boots, and a leather jacket.

Jamie leaped onto the bike like he'd been doing it for years. Tracie climbed aboard more gingerly. Then she slid ahead until her crotch was nestled against Jamie's taut butt and wrapped her arms around his lean waist.

"I'm beginning to see the appeal of this thing," she said through the microphone on her helmet. She gave her hips another wiggle and hugged him closer. Jamie's penis immediately hardened.

With a flourish of dust and stones, they were off. The bike did indeed ride smoother than Tracie had expected.

Before long, they had entered the freeway, and Jamie opened up the throttle. Over his shoulder, Tracie could see that they were going nearly a hundred miles an hour.

"If you ever hope to get me back onto this bike, you'll slow down," she warned.

"Where's the fun in that?" Jamie asked.

They were whistling by cars and trucks so fast the vehicles seemed to blur. Tracie got to experience the Doppler effect up close. Tracie felt like nothing lay between her and the road. It was at the same time a frightening and exhilarating feeling.

After an hour, Jamie pulled the bike onto a scenic overlook. The road seemed to drop away into a deep gully. At the bottom, sheep and cattle grazed, oblivious to the traffic above them. Jamie put the bike on its kickstand, and together they raced to the shade of a live oak tree.

"I must confess," Tracie said, "all that throbbing between my legs is a huge turn-on. I think I may have come in my pants."

"Well, we need to check that out," Jamie said as he undressed her. "I can't have you frustrated. It would spoil your ride."

In no time, they had stripped each other. The fresh air and the pounding of the engine had been exquisite foreplay. They fell on each other and had instant, rough sex.

Spent, they talked about Jamie's motorcycle dreams. "I've always wanted to travel the Million Dollar Highway," he admitted.

"Why do they call it that?" Tracie asked. "Is it because it cost a million dollars?"

"Closer than you think," Jamie agreed. "The stretch of road got its name from the high cost of construction. Builders had to literally cut the road through the treacherous Red Mountain

Pass between Ouray and Silverton. The time to complete it was significant."

"Is that the only reason?" Tracie asked.

"Well, another story goes that Million Dollar Highway comes from the gold and silver deposits that still lie buried beneath the highway," Jamie added.

"So, if we decided to do this trip, where would be start?"

Jamie pulled out his phone and located a map showing the route. "One of my buddies did this last year," he told Tracie.

They both bent over the phone. "He started at Durango first thing in the morning, just as the sun was rising. He aimed his BMW R1100RT north toward Silverton. Since he'd been riding over a lot of flat land to get there, he had to shift his thinking from flat, straight desert and prairie roads as he crossed into Colorado. He was now on extremely twisty mountain road. He said it was easy to get distracted by the beautiful alpine scenery."

"That sounds nice," Tracie said. "I could get used to steep, winding roads," she crooned, blowing in Jamie's ear.

"It's fifty miles to Silverton. But we'll take time to pull over and take some photos, relax, enjoy the view, and smell the wildflowers."

"Sure," Tracie murmured. "Enjoy the wild flowers... and the out-of-the-way places to... uh... rest."

"Right," said Jamie, momentarily distracted. With an effort, he returned to the route.

"Silverton is really isolated," he said. "It sits in a glacial valley surrounded by 13,000-foot high mountains. The town has only five hundred residents. It's 9,200 feet above sea level. Winters are rough. They get at least 300 inches of snow. Summer is high tourist season and the roads are busy."

Tracie was only half listening as she played with Jamie's belt buckle.

"Your first sight of Silverton is from a crest high above it. You descend to the valley floor and drive down a wide main street. It's just like the set of the old TV show, Northern Exposure," he noted, showing her a picture.

Tracie looked at the photo but continued to run her fingers up and down Jamie's arm. She smiled seductively when she noticed a bulge tenting his leather pants.

"When we're there," Jamie continued, "we can have breakfast in the Grand Hotel."

"That sounds... grand," murmured Tracie. "Will they have rooms to rent at the Grand Hotel?" she asked.

"If they don't, we'll improvise," Jamie promised.

"Can you show me how to improvise now?" she asked.

"Lucky for you, I am up to the task," whispered Jamie, taking her clothes off.

CHAPTER SEVEN

Problems in Paradise

"Right on time!" Lottie commented as she waved Tracie over to her table. Lottie had chosen to meet at the Capital Grille inside the Capitol building on Paces Ferry Road. The attractive restaurant was full of businessmen having lunch. Clearly, Lottie was a regular, judging by the location of her table and the fact that staff and clientele stopped to greet her.

"I HOPE you don't mind my choosing the restaurant," Lottie said. "I hate eating dishes I can't even pronounce, from menus I can't even read."

"IT WILL BE nice to dine on dishes I recognize," agreed Tracie. "Jamie takes me to places where I have to guess at what he has ordered for me."

. . .

"Herb and I used to eat here when we were in the area," Lottie commented. "I miss discussing ranch problems with him."

"Did your husband run the ranch before he passed away?" Tracie asked.

"Not hardly," Lottie replied. "Herb was a rodeo star. His prize money bought the land, but Herb had no head for business and no interest in the running of an operation that is several thousand acres of prime ranch land. He liked to come home to the ranch between shows. He loved to show off the place to his rodeo friends. But beyond that, he left the day-to-day running of the place to me and a bunch of ranch hands."

"So, is it a cattle ranch, Mrs. Chambers?" asked Tracie.

"Please call me Lottie," the big woman said, tossing back her bourbon and branch and signaling the waiter to bring two. "We have several hundred head of Herford cattle. but the big moneymaker is the quarter horse breeding business. Do you ride, Tracie?"

"Well, Mrs.—Lottie—I never have, but I'd love to learn."

"Then you come on out to the ranch. Quarter horses are the nicest little mounts. They're smart and they're hard workers. Like a good hunting dog, they aim to please."

. . .

"Sounds like a great combination, Lottie," Tracie said, raising her drink and taking a generous mouthful. She sputtered and coughed.

"Pace yourself, girl," Lottie cautioned, giving her a healthy slap on the back. "That's Kentucky bourbon. It's meant to be sipped. What say we order and then we can talk?" she suggested, straightening her jacket. She raised a finger and a young, handsome waiter appeared.

"Two of the usual, Miss Lottie?" he asked.

Tracie stared at Lottie's outfit. This one was red suede. Lavish silver embroidery decorated the sleeves, lapels, and yoke. Rhinestones sparkled up and down the cuffs. Hand-tooled red leather boots and a matching red Stetson completed her ensemble. "You look wonderful, as always," Tracie commented.

"I don't go in for girlie outfits," Lottie commented. "Herb and I were cowboys—with glitz. It was part of his rodeo personality, and I always felt more comfortable in cowboy attire. I know there has been all sorts of buzz about Audra and me being a couple. And we are—a couple of old broads having adventures and a few laughs together. If that makes people gossip, then so be it. We've got the money and the good health to do as we please. I know our friendship drives Marilyn to distraction. She has pointed out to her mother-in-law on several occasions what the rumor mills are saying. Pay Marilyn no mind. She's got a reindeer up her butt."

. . .

"Well, I'm not at the top of her popularity list either," Tracie admitted, taking a careful sip of her drink. "She has condemned me to the ministrations of Avril Steele. I'm sure they both think there's no hope for me."

"She dressed you today, didn't she?" Lottie said, eying Tracie's prim navy suit and matching pumps.

"Do I look like a school marm or a nun?" Tracie asked.

"Pretty much," said Lottie. "Let me guess. They wanted you to look proper when representing the business with an important client?"

"That's exactly what I was told," Tracie agreed, laughing.

"Well, tell them the men all ogled your schoolgirl costume."

"I think I'll just save that information to share with Jamie."

"You do that. That precious boy could use a laugh or two. His parents are too intense, and they expect so much of him. He walks a narrow tightrope trying to keep them and the clients happy. And that brings us to the reason for my asking you to lunch."

Lottie took a stiff drink and continued. "Audra and I have been talking. She can't be seen as airing family laundry, but I can. We think you need a heads-up. We both like you and think you're good for our boy. We're shocked that he's had the good sense to choose a quality girl, after the bimbos he's dated. So we don't want Marilyn to scare you off. And she will try. You see, Marilyn has Jamie's wife all picked out. She has the right look. She's been to the right schools. Her parents have money, and she has the proper background. Marilyn has merely been waiting for Jamie to sow his wild oats so she can get on with the marriage."

"Oh," breathed Tracie.

"She's not Jamie's choice. Remember that. Your paths will cross, and we want you to be prepared."

"Thank you," Tracie whispered, taking another sip of her bourbon.

"And there's another thing," Lottie continued. "Spellman Financial is not on solid ground as an investment business. Alan is not the astute investor his father was. He has made some bad deals. Audra and I are keeping a keen eye on things. Spellmans will go to any lengths to save the business and uphold their reputation. Don't let them throw you to the wolves."

. . .

"I—uh—I'll keep that in mind," Tracie stammered.

"Just remember," Lottie said, cutting up the final morsel of her rib eye and popping it into her mouth, "Audra and I have your back. If anything seems not quite right, you tell us. And let's make plans for you to come out to the ranch and go riding real soon."

With a wave, Lottie crawled into her classic Cadillac convertible and was on her way. "She's larger than life and a good person to have your back," Tracie said to herself as her car pulled up.

8

CHAPTER EIGHT

Whips and Riding Boots

Tracie strode from the bathroom. She stood tall and foreboding in her four-inch stilettos, the leather of her thigh-high boots shining in the moonlit bedroom. Her breasts swelled out the top of her leather bustier.

"Is this really what you want, Jamie?" she asked, picking up her whip.

JAMIE COULD SCARCELY SPEAK as he gazed up at his wife. His taut muscles bulged as he strained against the fur-lined handcuffs that he'd insisted Tracie use to bind his wrists and ankles to the bedposts. The Terminator tattoo on his chest seemed to writhe in pleasure as Jamie strained in anticipation of what was to come.

. . .

"I've been a bad boy," he whimpered. "Punish me! Make me your love slave."

Since Jamie raised the fantasy of femdom—dominatrix sexual fantasy—Tracie had done a lot of reading. Jamie had had a lot more sexual experiences than she had, and his fantasies were a great deal more lurid than hers.

Last night, he'd indulged her wishes, with the agreement that tonight was his night. Her mind traveled back to the evening before. Jamie had sprinkled rose petals on her bed. He'd approached her dressed only in an apron and a chef's hat and proceeded to create a sundae on her bare torso. When he'd topped the whipped cream with thick dark chocolate syrup and a cherry, he'd proceeded to lick off every ounce of the rich concoction—including some areas she was pretty sure that hot syrup had never penetrated. Then he had bathed her in bubbly, icy champagne and sucked up the residue.

Finally, they'd made wild, passionate love until the wee hours of predawn, falling asleep in a mass of tangled legs and arms. Tracie's core still tingled with the memory of the chilled champagne cascading over her burning body.

Now it was time for Tracie to make Jamie's dreams a reality. She hoped she was up to the task. What she'd learned from her research might not be equal to actual experience, but it would have to suffice.

She'd gotten strange looks at the bookstore when she'd purchased Henry Spencer Ashbee's *Index Librorum Prohibitorum*. But it revealed how the dominatrix existed as far back as 1877, in its first printing. The librarian was shocked when she checked out Anne Norris' *The History and Art of the Dominatrix*.

ALWAYS CURIOUS ABOUT THE UNKNOWN, Tracie immersed herself in the book. She discovered that the author was no teller of steamy romance. Born in the Antipodes, Norris received her MA degree in comparative art and archaeology. She presently worked as a historian, consultant, and curator on ancient and contemporary art. Norris took on clandestine training in one of Australia's leading dungeons, receiving instruction from fifteen dominatrices over a four-year period.

TRACIE DECIDED that this was as close to firsthand instruction as she was prepared to get. She discovered that "discipline" by physical punishment had religious connections. She also learned that disciplining religious impulses became eroticized in feminine dominance. The term *dominatrix* first appeared in the writings of Hrosvitha of Gandersheim in the 1600s. Medical research on human anatomy showed evidence of libido-lifting buttock beating. The image of the whip-wielding mistress painted female sex as a major erotic twentieth-century image.

IN OTHER REFERENCES, Tracie found evidence of both the term dominatrix and evidence of female-dominated sexual punishment as far back as the Middle Ages. Canoness Hrosvitha lived from 935 to 975 in Gar, Dersheim. In a late tenth-century manuscript, she outlined dominatrix techniques. The history of the dominatrix was argued to date back to rituals of the Goddess Inanna in Roman times. However, Tracie was most interested to learn that domination was showing a resurgence, particularly in the Western world.

Perhaps Jamie's fantasy sex isn't so far-fetched after all? she mused. Realizing that knowing the history of dominatrix wasn't getting her any closer to becoming good at it, Tracie turned her research to techniques.

Not wishing to attract more attention and gossip by visiting the library, Tracie turned to the internet. She soon discovered others in her position who were eager to share their knowledge.

She made a list of things she'd need to acquire:

Vinyl gloves. She learned that—for presentation—the preferable color was black. She also discovered that you could add "shine" by slicking these with Vaseline. Besides making your character look completely "hot," the gloves would help keep her manicure untouched when she got into some gnarly body orifices. This information gave her pause. Somehow, she figured being a dominatrix was all about ships and handcuffs.

Next, she learned that she and Jamie needed to have a safety word or phrase. Her domination needed to have limits. Although their first encounter might be gentle, experienced couples who chatted with her told her things would most likely become more intense as they progressed. They warned her not to go too far at first and to establish a safe word or phrase she and Jamie would be able to remember and recognize as "the safe word" in the heat of the moment.

Then she needed to investigate restraints. Couples told her these were a great way to start off. Jamie had given her fur-lined handcuffs. But zip ties, ropes, silk scarves, and ties were also suggested. She decided to start with the handcuffs and experiment with other things later.

Tracie's research also outlined the use of clamps. Many couples hated these things that she could clamp to Jamie's nipples or his scrotum. She was squeamish at the very thought, but Jamie already had a nipple ring—unbeknownst to his parents. So Tracie figured the idea of clamps might be something for down the road. Couples who used clamps said clothespins worked well, for starters. But she could also get metal clamps at any sex shop or online.

The next thing she looked into was gags. These might be as simple as duct tape or a silk scarf. If they wanted to use them, they could get a ball gag or a bite gag at any sex shop. Some couples advocated no gag, as the screaming and pleading were a turn-on for both members.

Candles were also a must to consider. Dribbling hot wax across Jamie's tattooed chest appealed to Tracie—as long as it didn't leave blisters he'd have trouble explaining at work.

Jamie had given Tracie a short whip with multiple switches on the end. Each had a metal end. Some couples advocated using a cat o' nine tails—a long whip with nine long lashes. Others liked to use an actual riding crop or paddles. They all told her buying real leather whips or paddles was worth the money. For the time being, Tracie decided to use the long whip Jamie had given her.

Down the road, Tracie was told, they might like to consider a dedicated room or "dungeon" for their sexual fantasies. If this were the case, they said a closet or coatrack containing things like floggers, ropes, chains, whips, and gags was a must. For the time being, Tracie decided the dark corner of her cavernous closet was just fine. "Nobody ever goes back there except me," she said to herself, forgetting about her maid, who hung everything up and kept her clothes in good repair, and Avril, who combed her hangers for the least objectionable outfit for Tracie's social obligations.

Tracie looked at pictures of some couples' private dungeons. She saw cages, walls with chains, and restraints. One looked like actual medieval dungeon. Another was centered around an Inquisition-style cage in a room lined in red velvet and satin brocade. Another had walls and ceilings of mirrors. They were all aimed at creating a fantasy world, cut off from reality.

For the time being, Tracie focused on how to use her costume, whips, restraints, and words to achieve Jamie's sexual fantasy. She was nervous because she knew dominatrices had been part of Jamie's sexual history, so they weren't novices in this S&M venture, exploring and growing together. She had to be good right out of the box.

KNOWING THIS, Tracie took a deep breath and called a number she'd been given for advice in becoming a competent, convincing dominatrix. She was given an address and a ten-o'clock appointment.

THE WOMAN who answered the door of the unassuming bungalow on a quiet, tree-lined street was a complete surprise to Tracie. Rosie was a petite, strawberry blonde with an hourglass figure. Dressed in black tights and an oversized T-shirt, she looked like a college freshman and moved like a ballerina.

TRACIE EXPLAINED her dilemma to Rosie. "You're smart to do your homework," Rosie said, offering her a large mug of coffee. "Let's see what I can add to what you've already learned. First, any kind of sex—including S&M—isn't a performance art. It's a shared activity. You've already shared a bed and sex, so you're in an enviable place. Much of the jitters will be gone. Remember: your anxiety will be obvious. You're trying something new. But you know it's something your partner wants, and he knows you want to help him realize his fantasy.

"So it's all good if I'm not as good as the dominatrices he's had before?" Tracie worried.

"Don't worry about them. Having you as his dominatrix is his fantasy. Having you wear the costume he bought you is part of his sexual dream. This isn't a contest. Relax and enjoy the shared experience."

"Jamie is my first sexual partner," Tracie admitted. "For me, sex is a whole new world. I spent my teen years avoiding sexual overtures from the hormone-crazed boys in my neighborhood and at my high school. I saw how premarital sex ruined the lives of the girls around me and trapped them in Skunk's Hollow forever, pregnant and poor. I vowed I'd get out of there. Avoiding sex was one of the things I did to protect that goal."

"I can see where you'd get that attitude toward sex," Rosie said, idly fingering the sparkling diamond in her nose. "But things have changed. Now, sex should be fun, an adventure. Your future is secure. You've got a partner who is intent on pleasuring you and who shares his sexual appetites with you. Sex isn't good or bad," she said. "It's just something you and your partner choose to do—like eating out or going dancing or surfing. Forget about the morality or monogamy issue. Just have fun exploring new horizons together. Don't get hung up on the fact that your partner has had other sexual partners. 'Not experienced' should not even be a part of your vocabulary. I've never flown a plane but 'not a pilot' is not how I describe myself. Sex, like horseback riding or playing tennis, is just something you and your partner opt to do together. Drop all those bullshit hang-ups. They're giving you performance anxiety."

"You're right," Tracie admitted. That's exactly what I have. So, how do I initiate the scene?"

"Be yourself," Rosie advised. "Get dressed up all sexy. Lots of glam and glitter. Have a quiet dinner at home or go out for a nice dinner. Try things like feeding each other morsels of food."

"I can do that," Tracie confirmed. "Then change into your costume and lead your partner to bed."

So, that's how Tracie found herself standing over her partner, who was hog-tied to the four-poster bed. With a deep breath, she transitioned herself into the dominatrix role. She'd read how Roman women used to have sex slaves, so she decided to work that fantasy with Jamie. By the looks of his engorged penis and his heavy breathing, he was totally up for their role play.

First, she used a long feather to tickle Jamie in all sorts of areas. She touched the inside of his ears with her feather. She brushed his eyelids gently. She tickled his lips and the inside of his nose until she made him sneeze. Then she descended and tickled his erect nipples. He writhed in agony at her touches, heaving his bound body to get more. Then she trailed the feather down his torso. Ignoring his eager penis, she began to stroke his scrotum with lightning-soft brushes. Jamie groaned and strained, his penis waving helplessly in the air, begging for her attention.

THEN SHE RETRACED her path up his torso, around his nipples, around his neck and tracing the orifices of his face. Jamie's skin gleamed with sweat, and the tattoo on his chest seemed to take on a life of its own as he heaved against his restraints.

Blowing out one of the candles that illuminated the room, Tracie carefully tipped hot wax onto Jamie's chest. With a gloved finger, she led the wax down his torso to his scrotum. Jamie moaned in pleasure at the touch of the hot wax and the silky smoothness of her gel-coated finger. Now it was time to get creative.

ADDING VASELINE, Tracie slipped a finger gently under Jamie's scrotum. Kneeling over him, her breasts straining at her black leather bustier, she slid her finger under his hips, circling his anus. Remembering how he had cock-teased her the night of her deflowering, she approached his sphincter muscle and just applied light pressure to the opening. Jamie went wild, pitching, moaning, and straining at his handcuffs.

WITH PRACTICED FLICKS of her whip, Tracie stimulated Jamie's penis until it was purple and throbbing. The veins stood out along the shaft. Deciding that was enough domination for their first experience, Tracie lay atop her partner, facing opposite ends of the bed, and began to lap his pulsing penis. She positioned herself so that Jamie could just reach her sweet spot. With much sucking and suckling, they both came in a crescendo. A giant wave of release left them weak.

TRACIE LAY where she was for five minutes and then crawled across the bed to release Jamie's restraints. "Was it good for you?" she murmured.

"THE BEST," Jamie whispered as they curled around one another and fell into a deep, satisfied sleep.

WHEN THEY AWOKE the next morning, Tracie stripped off her leather gear and placed it back in the dark corner of her closet. She deposited the feather, handcuffs, gloves, and boots into the large box below the bustier. When she emerged from the closet, Jamie was standing by the side of the bed. All of his muscles were erect, and he wore a wide grin.

"Let's finish what we started in the shower," he suggested. "I've been a very bad boy. I need to be washed out with soapy water... every part of me."

GIGGLING LIKE SCHOOLCHILDREN, they raced each another to the shower, where the combination of slippery soap, steaming jets of water, and the other's touch ended in stand-up sex in the roomy shower. Afterward, as they dried each other thoroughly with fluffy yellow towels and air blasting from the hair dryer, they talked about the previous night's experience.

. . .

"How did you get so good at your dom role?" Jamie asked.

"I read a lot," admitted Tracie. "And I got some excellent advice."

"Well, you certainly applied what you learned well," Jamie said, kissing her. "You were amazing!"

"I still have some tricks up my sleeve," Tracie murmured, blushing.

"I think we should consider sharing all this newfound talent of yours," Jamie said. "What would you think about inviting another couple to join us?"

"What do you mean?" Tracie asked. "You mean share our bedroom?"

"No," said Jamie. "I was actually thinking of building us a playroom. You think about it. Right now, we need to think about packing. One of our biggest clients, Percival Wrigley, has invited us to a party on board his yacht. Percival isn't very happy about Spellman Financial right now. It's just a misunderstanding about investment strategies. But I need a huge favor."

. . .

"What can I do to help?" Tracie asked. "I don't even know this man."

"You met him at the cocktail party. He was the one having the heated disagreement with my father."

"I believe he brushed by me on his way out the door," Tracie confirmed.

"Yes, that was Percival. So, I need you to charm him at this party. We've been asked to spend the night aboard the yacht with a few other guests. Before we dock the next day, I need you to use your talents to put Percival in a good mood."

"And what do you propose I do to accomplish that?" Tracie asked, picking up a bagel and smothering it with cream cheese.

"Whatever it takes, babe," Jamie said, kissing her ear. "Spellman Financial cannot afford to lose this high-profile client. We're in a mess here, and I am counting on you."

What next? Tracie wondered. The crispy bagel seemed to catch in her throat, and the raisin-cinnamon smell made her feel nauseous. *Is this really what it seems? Am I being pimped out?*

CHAPTER NINE

Lady in Red

When the limo that had been dispatched to take them and two other couples to the yacht arrived at the marina, the party was in full swing. Tracie felt relaxed in spite of the fact that Marilyn and Alan Spellman were two of the people who traveled to the yacht with them.

Things had never warmed up between her and Marilyn, but it was as if Marilyn had been warned to be cordial tonight. It might also have been because the other couple in the limo was the new accountant and his young wife, a runway model. Fascinated with the slim brunette's career, Tracie had asked her a lot of questions, and the ride from the hotel to the dock had gone quickly.

Marilyn had taken one look at Tracie's new red dress and red stiletto shoes and had glared at Jamie. Alexa and Ronald had both commented that Tracie looked ravishing. Tracie thanked them and remarked that the outfit was a gift from Jamie. This prompted another glare from his mother.

Unfazed, Jamie pointed out that the dress was a business investment.

"Well," replied his father, smiling and downing his second glass of champagne. "It's a good one."

Marilyn elbowed her husband in the ribs when she thought no one was looking.

At the gangway, the crew, dressed in crisp white shirts and dark trousers, took Tracie's and Jamie's luggage to their stateroom, and the six guests were shown on board and given brimming glasses of sparkling pink champagne in which fresh raspberries bounced up and down.

The conversation got louder as alcohol flowed and guests helped themselves to the lavish buffet.

When Tracie was introduced to their host, Percival acknowledged, "I met you at that cocktail thing at the Spellmans'. Then I was one of the two thousand guests at your wedding."

"I remember," Tracie said, holding out her hand. Instead of shaking it, Percival pulled her close and kissed her outstretched palm. "We'll get a lot better acquainted later when we deposit this lot back on dry land," he promised. A twinge of apprehension ran up her spine.

"I'm looking forward to it," she answered, managing a wobbly smile. After all, Jamie was counting on her.

Throughout the evening, Jamie continued to work the crowd. Left to her own devices, Tracie drank too much champagne. Conversations got funnier as her vision began to blur. The later it got, the more overt were the glances and touches from the men at the party. Tracie felt as if she were back at high school—only wearing nicer clothes. Fortunately, she still remembered how to fend off unwanted interest.

By far the most overt attention came from their host. Tracie tried to treat his hands roving on her body and his whispered hot breath in her ear as lightly as she could, without being rude.

After all, he was their host and a very big client. And Jamie had asked her to charm Percival. Besides, she liked the way the smooth-talking man's attention so obviously enraged Marilyn Spellman. A couple of times, her grim-faced mother-in-law had started toward her, only to have Alan Spellman pull her back. It seemed that he was aware of her conversation with Jamie and of what she was expected to do for the business.

Eventually, the yacht docked and the guests who had not been invited to spend the night were shuttled off to waiting limousines. As she passed by Tracie on her way out, Marilyn hissed, "Behave yourself and don't embarrass our family."

Tracie smiled sweetly at Marilyn and whispered, "Just enhancing the corporate image, Mother Spellman."

Marilyn shot daggers at her.

"Let's get you safely off to your room, little lady," a silky voice said as Tracie listed to the left. She felt strong arms picking her up, and everything went black.

With a lurch, Tracie came to her senses. Her dress was neatly folded on a chair. Her shoes were lined up in front of the dress. She moved the sheet and realized she was wearing nothing. Her head ached and her mouth felt as if someone had stuffed it with steel wool. She recalled champagne—bottles of it. But this was more disturbing than a hangover. Everything felt off. The room was strange. The walls seemed to be leaning. Her bed felt tipped. And, try as she might, she could recall nothing of the party the evening before, beyond Marilyn Spellman's hissing at her as she left the yacht.

The yacht! Tracie breathed a sigh of relief.

That would explain the gentle rocking motion and the strange room.

But, where is Jamie? And who undressed me? And how did my clothes get folded so neatly?

With a lurch, Tracie managed to get upright. She placed a

shaky hand on the wall and moved gingerly toward the bathroom. Perhaps a cold shower would revive her and jog her memory.

Standing in the steamy shower with one hand propping her up, Tracie lathered herself with jasmine-scented soap and let the water wash over her. Her hands worked the blue loofa across her aching body. She was sore in places that only rough lovemaking could reach.

What in hell happened last night? she wondered. No details materialized. On the one hand, she thirsted for information. On the other hand, she hoped she'd never recall the past evening's events.

She'd had hangovers before—far too many of them since becoming Tracie Spellman. But she'd always been able to recall what had transpired during her drunken partying. To have a complete blank slate surrounding last night was terrifying. *What if I'd done something horrible?*

Finding nothing else to wear, Tracie donned her red dress from the evening before and, carrying her impossibly high shoes, skittered down the passageway to her own room.

In whose room did I spend the night? she wondered again, slipping the key card into the slot on her door. *Lucky these cards come with room numbers*, she mused. *I wonder how many others would have difficulty locating their stateroom otherwise?*

She half expected to see Jamie here, but there was no sign of him except for the rumpled bed and the wet towels on the bathroom floor. But he hadn't been gone for long, if the still-steamed bathroom mirror was any indication.

Taped to her luggage, Tracie found a note.

Well done, my love! Percival can't wipe the contented look off his face. Meet me in the dining room as soon as you get this. We've got a bit of a situation.

She wondered what Jamie meant by "a situation." Hadn't she

fixed the situation? His note would seem to indicate that. *What other situation could there be?*

At Jamie's mention of Percival Wrigley, Tracie recalled their pre-party conversation in which Jamie had asked Tracie to "charm" Percival into leaving his money invested with the Spellmans. The phrase "whatever it takes" lingered in her recall.

Tracie pulled her hair back and clipped it atop her head. She pulled a casual outfit from the tiny closet where the staff had hung her clothes and added a dab of makeup.

Lucky for me, there was no one in the corridor when I made my escape, she thought. *One look at my state of dishevelment and they'd have known immediately that I hadn't spent the night in my own room.*

Now that she thought about it, not seeing staff scurrying around and cleaning rooms was strange.

Giving her appearance one final appraisal, Tracie grabbed her tote and followed the signs to the dining room.

10

CHAPTER TEN

Man Overboard

Before she entered the dining room, Tracie was struck by the silence. While people sat in groups of six at the round, linen-covered tables, no one spoke. They all seemed to be in shock.

Spotting Jamie at a table with an empty chair, she slid into her spot, smiling shyly at the other six people at the table.

"What's going on?" Tracie whispered to Jamie, glancing around the room at the stony faces of the fifty people assembled there.

"I'll explain later," Jamie said, nodding at the podium at the front of the room.

There was a clicking sound as a tall, thin man in his forties tapped the microphone. He straightened his red tie and shot the french cuffs of his white shirt beyond the sleeves of his tailored navy suit. All eyes turned to him.

"Good morning, ladies and gentlemen," he said. "I'm Detective Baird with the San Diego Police. Last evening, at three fifteen, our dispatcher received a call that a passenger aboard this boat had disappeared. He was last seen having a heated discussion with another passenger shortly after two thirty. When his wife went to look for him, he was gone. Police and the coast guard were called. The crew has searched the ship and found no trace of him. It appears that he may have gone overboard. The coast guard is presently searching the water. Police will be questioning all passengers still on board. We've sent a team to question guests who left the boat after was docked. At this point in time, we haven't any more information. If you took photos on board last night, we are asking that they be emailed to this address." Detective Baird flashed an email address on the screen behind the podium.

"Our investigation team will be questioning each of you. Please provide as full an account of the proceedings here last evening. Everything—no matter how unrelated it may seem—will help us piece together what happened. I apologize for the inconvenience. We'll get you on your way as quickly as possible. The captain has set up a boardroom where we can conduct our investigation. In the meantime, please sit tight. Thank you."

As guests were led to be questioned, Tracie turned to Jamie. "Who is missing?" she asked. "Is this the situation you mentioned in your note?"

"It seems that Howard Rich has vanished," Jamie told her. He wore a lazy smile, as if he found the whole thing entertaining.

"Isn't that the guy you and your father had the huge blowup with over a client he stole from you?" Tracie asked.

"Oddly enough," Jamie replied, "we had a rather heated discussion in the wee hours last night. It seems old Howard is wangling to get Percival's business, hinting that our methods are not completely aboveboard."

Tracie's eyes grew wide. "You are the one he was arguing with? Do the police know?"

"If they don't, I'm sure the grief-stricken wife will have filled them in. At best, I'm a person of interest. At worst, I'm their prime suspect for whatever they think happened to Howard."

"You seem amazingly calm about all of this," Tracie noted. "Did anyone see you after your discussion?"

"When Howard and I finished talking, I had a double scotch at the bar and went to our room. The rest of the night—what little remained of it—is a blur. At six this morning, we were all rousted from our rooms and shuffled into the dining room. I've called the old man and alerted him to a possible problem. His lawyers are on their way. Until they arrive, I'm to say nothing."

"This whole thing is like living inside a murder mystery," Tracie said. "How did I miss the call to come to the dining room?"

"I suspect the owner of this fair ship was protecting your reputation—and his—when he failed to mention you were sharing his stateroom," Jamie replied, smiling. "Even this disappearing act Richie Rich has pulled can't wipe the satisfied look off Percival's face. He looks like the old tomcat that was just served a dish of cream. You must have been magnificent."

"So you're good with Percival?" Tracie asked, strangely proud of the part she'd played in helping her husband's business.

"Oh, I think, with your charming performance and Howard's fortuitous disappearance, Percival will be happy to stay with us."

CHAPTER ELEVEN

Person of Interest

After the Spellman lawyers arrived on the scene, Jamie was questioned by the police. He was told that he was a person of interest because of the heated conversation the evening before.

"What were you arguing about?" Detective Baird asked him.

Pausing to get a nod from his lawyers, Jamie replied, "Howard and I were having an animated discussion about business. You know we are both in investments. We'd both had a lot to drink, I must confess, and our talk may have gotten loud and distracted the merriment of our fellow guests. When I went to the bar for a nightcap, Howard remained on deck. His balance wasn't too steady. I cautioned him not to get too close to the rail. I won't tell you what his reply was."

"When was this?" the detective asked, scanning his notes.

"I'd guess between two thirty and three," Jamie replied. "I really didn't check my watch."

"Can anyone corroborate your whereabouts?" Detective Baird asked, staring at Jamie knowingly.

"The bartender can attest to when I left the dining room. After that, I crashed in my room… alone. The cameras in the corridors and when I swiped my room card should tell you the rest."

"What did they ask?" Tracie said, biting her lower lip when Jamie returned. "What will they ask me?"

"Just tell them exactly what happened," Jamie told her. "Give them as many details as you can recall."

"Well, that's just it," Tracie said, worrying a thumbnail. "I don't recall much of anything after your mother left. Percival brought me a drink, and the rest of the night is a complete blank."

"So you don't remember anything about your romp with old Percy?" asked Jamie. "Pity! I was hoping for details."

When Tracie returned from questioning, she said, "They asked me why I wasn't in my room until eight this morning."

"What did you tell them?"

"I said I was meeting with one of my husband's business clients, and we lost track of time. I passed out and have no recollection of where I was or what I did until twenty to eight this morning. I admitted I'd had a lot to drink and much of the evening was a blur. They asked me if I'd witnessed the argument between you and Howard."

"What did you tell them?" Jamie asked.

"The truth. You were busy talking with clients, and I was pretty much left to my own devices. If you had a discussion with this man, I didn't notice or I had already left the party by then."

"That's good, babe," Jamie replied. "Unless they can produce witnesses or damning photos or a body, they haven't got much of a case. Who knows? Howard may have pulled a disappearing act. I heard he and his wife are having problems."

12

CHAPTER TWELVE

Oh, What a Tangled Web

Eventually, everyone was questioned and sent on their way. Jamie was instructed to make himself available should the police have more questions. He and his father seemed tense in the days that followed, but Tracie tacked that up to concerns about accounts of their biggest clients and to the fact that there was still no sign of Howard Rich.

While not warm and welcoming, Marilyn seemed grudgingly resigned to Tracie's place in the family. In spite of the uneasy truce between the two women, both avoided the other. Marilyn was kept busy with her charity fundraising projects, lunch at the country club, her personal trainer, and a round of golf once a week with her long-standing foursome.

Tracie was content to make meals, put the finishing touches on her new house, and sun by the pool. She'd taken Lottie up on her offer to ride. Both Jamie and his father were delighted that she was spending time with an important client.

Percival had called to apologize for having departed from his stateroom so hastily the morning Howard Rich went missing. He invited Jamie and her to dine aboard his yacht, and they'd had a pleasant time. No reference to what had transpired on their last visit had been mentioned. While he was an attentive host, Percival did not make overtures to Tracie.

Just as things seemed to be returning to normal, Jamie opened the paper one morning and whistled. "Whoa! What do we have here?"

Tracie glanced at the social section. There were photos of her and Jamie boarding the yacht. Then her eyes traveled to another, larger photo. "Who is the Mystery Guest?" the headline read. The caption identified the man leaning over the bed as billionaire financier Percival Wrigley. Clearly, there was a naked woman on the bed, but her face was hidden. The edge of a small rose tattoo peeked out of the sheet carelessly thrown over her.

Tracie and Jamie recognized the small rose tattoo. "Where did this come from?" Tracie asked in horror.

"Someone must have planted a camera in old Percy's room," Jamie said. "Chill out, babe. No one knows about that tattoo except you and me—and maybe Percival—if he wasn't too drunk or distracted to notice. It's fine. In fact, this photo might be good insurance that Percival won't soon be contemplating yanking his account from Spellman Financial. Whoever leaked this to the press may have done us a favor."

He walked down the hall, whistling. "Dad and I have a meeting this afternoon. We're meeting here because we want to avoid the press that has been sniffing around. Will you bring us coffee, babe? And stop worrying. You look like the kid who stole cookies from the cookie jar. Relax! Everything will work out just fine."

Still upset by the photo, Tracie busied herself in the kitchen setting out coffee things. She was just about to push open the door of the study and deliver the tray of coffee and snacks when she overheard the two men talking. She froze in her tracks.

"That was a great plan, Jamie. I've got to hand it to you. I was thinking about hiring a hooker to warm up old Percival. But using your wife as 'bait' for Percival? That was inspired. Who'd have thought you could get that girl to agree to charm old Percy. Is she that hot?"

"Dad, hot doesn't even begin to describe it. That girl will cream her pants before I lay a hand on her. That motorcycle I bought? Giant sex turn-on. She has an orgasm just hugging me and riding that machine. I told you she was a great find. She's already got Lottie eating out of her hand like one of her fancy horses. I can hardly wait to turn her lose on old Harold Hargrave."

"You're right. Old Hard Woody will get a stiffy just watching her moves. When can we set that up?" asked Jamie's father. "We've got to make sure our big accounts are secure before that ass Howard Rich gets back on the scene."

"I know, Dad, but I don't want to push too hard. I want to keep some of that action for myself. Can't give it all away. Besides, I don't want Tracie to get suspicious."

"That's a good point. Hey! Are you still seeing that little secretary you set up in the condo in Macon?"

Jamie nodded. "She's been a good source of information on potential clients, working at the bank. But she's bucking for a promotion. If she leaves the investments department, she won't be as much use to us as she has been. Besides, she is making nesting noises again. And the fees just went up on that condo. I'm thinking it might be time to cut our losses there."

"Whatever you think, son. You've always had a good sense of timing with those contacts. I'll miss the action I was getting with her, though. She was far enough away that your mother didn't know anything about her, and yet, an easy drive when I was supposed to be at a conference."

"Any blowback from the missing Howard Rich?" asked Jamie.

"Our lawyers say the police are tabling that case. It's hard to charge someone when there's no body and no evidence of foul play."

"I'd be very surprised if they ever find a body," Jamie said. "Those waters are full of sharks. If a drunk fell overboard, he'd be shark meat before he sank to the bottom. Nothing left out there except a Rolex!"

"How'd you get him over the railing?" asked Alan.

"Piece of cake! Drugged his drink. Flipped him over as he was passing out, then continued to play the shouting match for another ten minutes. Came back inside shouting a final argument at where people thought Howard was still standing. Then had a scotch nightcap and off to bed. My key card and the cameras in the hall were my alibi."

"I hope I never get on the wrong side of you, son," said his father.

"Not as long as you're signing my checks, Dad."

"So how much longer are we going to need your wife?" asked Alan. "Your mother is making a big fuss about Tiffany again."

"Tell Mom to cool her jets. Tiffany is never going to be as useful to us as Tracie is. Besides, Audra and Lottie like her. We don't want to piss them off!"

"No. That's for sure. Your grandmother still scares the shit out of me. And as for that Amazon friend of hers? I shudder to think what she'd do to us."

"When Tracie goes, it will have to be her idea. We can't risk bad press."

"Speaking of the press," Alan said, "how did they get their hands on those Percival tapes?"

"You mean from the cameras I installed in his stateroom?" asked Jamie.

"You put those cameras in there?"

"Of course. I wanted to see what was happening. The idea of leaking a shot where the girl's face isn't visible came to me later. It's insurance against Percival in case he decides to take his business elsewhere."

"I've got to hand it to you, son. You've got a shrewd mind, just like your grandfather."

"I'm sorry I never got a chance to meet him," Jamie commented. "He must have been something."

"He was something. That's for sure. Meanest old son of a bitch you'd ever want to meet. He'd cheat his own grandmother. And he didn't hesitate to beat us over the smallest things he deemed infractions. The husband Audra likes to paint for the public is not the father I remember. I don't blame her for taking up with Lottie. I'd have sworn off men, too, if I'd been her. The business would not be still standing if Mother hadn't poured her inheritance into it."

"I wonder if Tracie has forgotten about the coffee," Jamie remarked.

"You asked her to bring it down here?" he father exclaimed. "What if she heard us talking?"

"Chill out, Dad. Tracie adores me. And so what if she heard us talking? It's not like a wife can testify against her husband."

"If you *were* her husband," Alan reminded him.

"Well, there's that," Jamie admitted. "I don't like to think what would happen if Tracie ever guessed our wedding was sheer fiction."

"The things we do to keep Marilyn happy!" exclaimed Alan. "You know she still expects you to marry that socialite?"

"We'll cross that bridge when we come to it," Jamie replied. "Tiffany is too prim and proper to make an interesting wife. I have some plans that the straightlaced Tiffany would never agree to. Tracie hasn't outlived her usefulness yet. Tiffany will always be available if we need her pedigree and her father's millions. Mother will see to that."

"So what are these plans?" Alan asked.

"Well, I'm thinking of turning the basement into an S&M dungeon of sorts," Jamie said. "I broached the idea of inviting another couple, and Tracie didn't say no. She seemed only concerned that it not happen in our bedroom."

"You lucky SOB!" exclaimed Alan. "It'd be a hot day in December before I ever got Marilyn to agree to anything other than the missionary position, once a month. There's a reason you're an only child."

"Too much information, Dad," Jamie shuddered.

"So who do you have in mind? Anyone I know?"

"Well, as a matter of fact, Tracie seemed to hit it off with your new accountant's wife."

"The one with the great legs?" asked Alan.

"I thought we'd feel them out and see what they had to say," suggested Jamie. "Any problems with that?"

"Why would I have a problem?" asked Alan.

"Well, Ronald works for us. If it doesn't work out, it could make things a little sticky at work."

"No problem. If it doesn't work out, we can always come up with some reason to fire him. It's not without precedent. Remember those secretaries you dated?"

"Now that I think about it," remarked Jamie, "they aren't there anymore."

"Exactly," said his dad. "Is there anything else we need to discuss?"

"I could use a cup of coffee."

Just then, there was a tap at the door. Jamie opened it to find Tracie balancing a large tray with coffee cups, a coffee pot, and a plate of cookies. "Sorry I took so long," she said with a smile. "The tray was heavy."

Her mind whirled as she deftly poured coffee and passed homemade chocolate chip cookies. When she returned to the kitchen, she picked up the phone and dialed. A raspy voice answered. "Lottie," said Tracie, "we need to talk."

SIGN UP TO RECEIVE FREE BOOKS

Sign Up to Receive Free E-Books and Audiobook Codes.

Would you like to read **The Unexpected Nanny, Dirty Little Virgin** and **other romance books** for **free**?

You can sign up to receive these free e-books and audiobooks by typing this link into your browser:

https://www.steamyromance.info/free-books-and-audiobooks-hot-and-steamy/

Or this one:

https://www.steamyromance.info/the-unexpected-nanny-free/

PREVIEW OF FIRST LOVE
A SINGLE DAD NEXT DOOR ROMANCE

By Celeste Fall

Blurb

Thirty-four-year-old Clay Booth had it all: a satisfying career, tons of money, a son he loved to distraction, and all the female attention he wanted. After a tumultuous marriage ended in Parker's mother's suicide, Clay vowed to have nothing but meaningless sex. However, he had not reckoned on the allure of smart, breathtakingly beautiful Virginia Matthew, the naïve, virginal girl next door. Clay's pursuit of her was complicated by the fact that the owner of his building—Virginia's promiscuous mother—was stalking him. Will his crush on Virginia make him break his promise to have no meaningful relations with women? To what lengths will Clay to make this young virgin happy?

"MY SISTER WARNED me to stay away from the trusting girl next door

However, what she didn't factor in to this situation was that I'd fall head over heels in love with this girl. Her hot skin tantalized my sleep. Her moist, luscious lips begged for mine to wed hers when I tried to concentrate at work. I could hear her tinkling laugh in my dreams. How can I get out from under her spell? What am I going to do? There's no happy ending in sight, no matter which path I take."

"Wow! This is no boy next door. Clay Booth is all man. Every time he fixes me with those piercing, blue eyes, I go all soft inside. My body yearns for him at night. My dreams are filled with hot, sweaty images of him kissing me all over. I think about him night and day. Those soft, exciting lips beckon me to discover regions I've never dreamed about. I feel like such a naughty girl. What's happening to me? Mother warned me that this would not end well. Alas! For once, mother could be right.

CHAPTER ONE

Deanna Matthews fluffed her artfully-streaked blonde hair and straightened the jacket of her Chanel suit. She smiled at her reflection in the mirror of her penthouse apartment. Taking an atypical moment to self-reflect, Deanna looked around the tastefully-appointed apartment and allowed herself to feel proud of her success. When her marriage had ended in a nasty divorce nearly sixteen years ago, Deanna had swallowed the shame of being the jilted wife and looked for a way to provide a good life for herself and her young daughter, Virginia, then a shy six-year-old.

Walking over to the balcony, Deanna stepped outside and surveyed the stunning view from her home. Even from here, she could see the Matthews and Martin Realty billboards that graced benches, buses, and buildings throughout Panama City Beach. Her photograph on them was ten years old and in need of an update, but nevertheless ...

I still look good. Her full lips, still filler-free, curved in another wide, trademark smile, the kind that many looked at and mistakenly judged to be naïvely trusting. Its owner, however, was anything but. Deanna was a survivor. On the heels of her acrimonious divorce, deserted by people she'd once considered friends, she had struck out entirely on her own. Through sweat and tears that her former acquaintances could never have fathomed, she'd formed a real estate partnership and earned the admiration of the business community. Twice voted local realtor of the year, she now owned the Sea Urchin Luxury Condominiums where she lived, amongst many other beachfront high rises.

Walking back inside, her eyes drifted to the mantle with the carefully shined awards she'd accumulated. At the back of the apartment, she heard the TV going, probably left on by a maid. A familiar voice caught Deanna's ear and she grimaced, realizing it was *that* hour. Exactly at this time, every day for over twenty years, her ex, Bernie Matthews, dished out a daily dose of advice to needy housewives. He was Seattle's answer to Dr. Phil and Dr. Fraser Crane all rolled into one. Bernie, a licensed psychologist with only mediocre success in his practice, had carved out a career as a TV psychologist with his self-important, outspoken style. He had a niche market with the over-forties female viewing audience, which Deanna always found ironic as Bernie preferred his women half that age.

Even his voice was greasy. Deanna cringed at the thought that she had ever found him appealing. Bernie hadn't been a good husband. He hadn't even been a good father. He'd always been more concerned about his career than his family.

She walked away from the noise, heading toward the kitchen for the last dregs of her espresso. Instead of the tepid remains she'd expected, she found a fresh demi tasse laid out by one of her staff and made a mental note to remember the thoughtfulness at Christmas. Idly, she sipped the steaming brew and mused over the lack of contact between her only child and her ex.

It was just as well, Deanna thought, tapping perfect nails

against the gleaming, granite counter. Her philandering husband had always had a preference for younger women. If the Seattle social pages were any indication, that hadn't changed. Shy and awkward Virginia didn't need to be dragged into that rat's nest of social flurry. As extroverted as Deanna and Bernie were, it was no wonder Virginia had grown up to become the polar opposite of her gregarious, frequently bitterly at odds, parents.

As a result, probably, of seeing one too many louche soirees, Virginia now had few friends. Those she did have all shared an online interest in marine life—like that nerdy Arty Stone who, Deanna thought, was the epitome of the word *geek*. He and Virginia had never met in person—Deanna wasn't even sure where Arty lived. But, ever since Virginia had discovered a marine-life chatroom, she and Arty had been in daily contact.

Shaking off her momentary mood, Deanna shrugged. Yes, she admittedly had little room to criticize Bernie. Since the divorce, Deanna, tanned, toned, and looking at least a decade younger than her mid-fifties, had developed a taste for nubile, young men. She was discrete about it, but, after all, a girl had needs. Why not scratch that itch with someone attractive, energetic, and eager? Deanna's real estate business brought her in contact with a continuous supply of men with surfer bodies who wanted nothing more than she did: a quick, enthusiastic coupling with no strings attached.

Virginia was routinely horrified by her mother's 'cougar' antics—God, Deanna hated that word—but really, what was the harm? She had just sold the other penthouse to a tall, dark, and handsome, billionaire, Clay Booth. He was a touch more acerbic than most men she had briefly dated, but his looks made up for any lack in social graces. He didn't appear attracted to her yet— yet being the key. She had seldom met a man of any age who could resist her charms, and Deanna Matthews was not one to fold when a challenge arose.

She put her cup in the dishwasher, took the bottle of chilled champagne from its customary bucket, plucked two crystal flutes from the cabinet, and added a crystal dish of caviar and a bowl of chocolate-dipped strawberries from the fridge.

"Buckle up, big boy," she said as she walked out of her apartment and straight across the hall, to where Clay had bought the last unit in her building—at a seven-figure price—without even blinking. Deanna's commission on the sale would be mind boggling and she had every intention of celebrating.

She rang Clay's door bell and struck a seductive pose, murmuring, "Welcome to my world. Let the celebration begin."

CHAPTER TWO

Clay walked through his brand-new apartment, needing to traverse quite a distance to get to the front door. After seeing it on Skype, his ocean-obsessed son, who was the whole reason he'd bought the place, had joked that they needed to install "one of those walking sidewalk things." Clay hadn't disagreed.

He picked up the pace when the bell rang again, even though he didn't usually hurry for much of anybody—not since he'd earned his first billion. Ever since, the money had continued to roll in, and with it, people's automatic respect, a concept that still sometimes confused him. Walking past a glossy brochure on an equally glossy end table that the decorator had purchased, Clay's eyes moved over the Bay County tourism logo, the group for which he was now working with, marketing 'medical holidays' to northerners who needed age-related surgeries. The idea was they could get treatment in one of the country's fine medical facilities and convalesce in a condo facing the ocean. Clay's job was to work with the stakeholders and sell the idea in cities like Boston, New York, St. Louis, and Chicago.

It had all worked out well, he mused, nearing the door and taking a guess at who was behind the impatient buzzing. The penthouse at Sea Urchin was perfect. There were lots of room. It was private. It had state-of-the-art security. All in all, it was a win for medicine, a win for realty, a win for seniors ...

And a win for him, he congratulated himself as he answered the door and swept his eyes over Deanna Matthews' bombshell body. From the time Clay had strolled into the realty offices of Matthews and Martin, Clay had sensed Deanna was eager to offer more than real estate. *Yes,* he thought, eyeing the champagne and strawberries in her carefully manicured hands. *She is a full-service provider.*

She was just the type of woman Clay favored. Beautiful. No strings. No promises. Just hot, sweaty, loud, monkey sex.

"This is a nice surprise." His eyes swept the voluptuous Deanna from head to toe as he accepted the welcome basket. *Yummy,* he thought. He wasn't looking at the welcome basket.

"I had some last-minute paperwork for you to sign," purred Deanna as she slid by Clay. "So, I thought we'd kill two birds with one stone and toast your new home ...unless you're busy settling in."

"What's to settle in?" asked Clay. "The decorator did his bit. Her bit? I'm going to let Parker help decorate his room so it will feel more like home."

"His bit. When does Parker arrive?" asked Deanna, closing the door firmly behind her without invitation. "I'd love to meet him. Perhaps we can get together for dinner and he can meet my little girl, Virginia."

"PARKER IS FINISHING his school year in Houston," Clay explained. "I have him enrolled at Bay Academy for August."

"What's he interested in?" asked Deanna. "My little girl has some interesting hobbies. Is he excited about the move?"

He wondered about how little her daughter could be, when, as well-preserved as she was, Deanna was at least somewhere in the vicinity of 50. "He's not unexcited about it." Clay shrugged. "Parker's kind of moved around a lot because of my job. He's an odd kid with unusual interests. He won't miss Texas because he's not leaving friends. At the moment, he's consumed by facts about dolphins and sharks. Not your typical kid at all, so he has a hard time making friends."

"My daughter is working at Gulf World this summer," Deanna commented. "She's teaching dolphins to do something or other. Maybe they could get together and talk? Perhaps Virginia could even show Parker the dolphins."

"If she'd do that," said Clay. "I'd be forever in your debt."

"Let's crack open this champagne and sample this caviar. We can talk about how you can repay me over breakfast."

"Let me get that champagne popped open," Clay said easily, enjoying the moment, even though he wasn't about to climb bed with his realtor. Not a good business move, however much his lower half disagreed. He'd let her down gently, after they drank enough.

CHAPTER THREE

Deanna woke up the next morning in her own room, to an empty bed, but it didn't faze her. Much. While she was admittedly disappointed at having been gently but firmly put off by Clay the night before, the evening had, nevertheless, been an enjoyable one. Clay was nearly as good a conversationalist as Deanna imagined he would've been in bed. Not that she'd completely given up that hope; that wasn't how she'd (finally) gotten ahead in life.

Not one for lounging, she rolled out of bed and headed for the shower, thinking about her daughter again. Virginia would be returning from a rare visit to her dad's later this morning. Deanna hoped that this visit would be the beginning of more frequent visits to Bernie's. She wasn't sure what had prompted it, but it had given Deanna the freedom to pursue her fling with the hunky billionaire next door.

If it ever did happen, Deanna was under no illusions that her relationship with the bad boy next door would be anything but a glorious roll between the sheets. Her failed relationship with Bernie, the philanderer, had taught her to keep everything with men purely physical and fleeting. Clay was not the kind to put down roots. When he'd accomplished his mission in Panama City Beach, he'd be on to another lucrative challenge somewhere else.

So what? Deanna thought, scrubbing off beneath the pulsing rain shower. *That just means I'll get another fat commission for turning this condo over again. Win-win!*

Deanna wondered idly how all this moving affected his eight-year-old. She sympathized with Clay as a single parent, but considered whether Clay's single-minded attitude toward his work left his son with a lot of time spent with nannies and babysitters. She shrugged. Virginia had had sitters and nannies after they'd moved to Panama City Beach. She'd turned out just fine.

For a fleeting moment, Deanna wondered whether the celibacy her daughter had adopted had anything to do with the multiple couplings of her parents.

Did that part of our lives affect her too? How can a girl reach twenty-two and still be a virgin? Deanna wondered, reaching for a nearly-empty bottle of shampoo. *Is that normal?*

She gave up that train of thought as she soaped up her long hair, still almost completely naturally blonde, and began to think about various meetings she had scheduled for the day.

CHAPTER FOUR

Virginia balanced parcels and reached out to swipe the card in the elevator. It dropped on the floor and she muttered, "Damn!"

"Here. Let me get that for you!" a deep voice said. Over her packages, Virginia saw a tanned hand reach around her to swipe a card in the slot.

"Thank you!" Virginia peered over the top of her boxes— way over the top ...wow, he was tall—into the deepest, bluest eyes she had ever seen. "Hi," she squeaked. *I sound like a school girl,* she thought. *Not like a twenty-two-year-old, master's-level college student.*

"Can I help you with those?" asked the man, taking two boxes from her.

"Thanks," breathed Virginia, flexing her fingers where they tingled from brushing up against his. "They're brochures for a program at Gulf World. I have to fold them so they will be ready for Monday," she explained.

"And you're ...dropping them off here?" he asked, nodding at the now-open door to her mother's apartment. "Deanna said something about her little girl working at Gulf World. I didn't realize Deanna herself was involved in volunteering."

"She's not," Virginia said in confusion. "I am. I mean, I'm not. A volunteer. I mean ...wow." She had a tendency to get tongue-tied in the best of circumstances, but this was impressive even for her. Stepping past the gorgeous guy, she walked over to a brand-new coffee table and set her two boxes down, then walked back for the others.

He held them slightly away, eyebrows raised in a playful challenge.

She tried again. "I'm Virginia. Deanna's daughter. I work at Gulf World. And you're ..."

"Clay. *You're* Deanna's little girl?" There was more than a hint of disbelief in the man's tone, making Virginia laugh even as she processed the fact that this was the hunky billionaire her mother had been ranting and raving about for days.

"That's right. I'm finishing my master's in marine biology." *So eloquent, Virginia. God.*

"Not that I would ever question a lady's age, but ..."

"I'm twenty-two," she replied, taking his boxes from him. "Yes, I know, I'm not exactly little. Mom loves to describe me that way. It makes her feel maternal or something."

"I'd debate the not-little thing," Clay answered, leaning against the door jamb, long legs stretched out in front of him in a way that stretched his jeans just *so,* raising Virginia's virginal pulse several notches. "You're, what, one hundred pounds soaking wet?"

"You don't get to ask a lady both her age and her weight three minutes after meeting her," Virginia retorted, grateful to find that her elevated hormone levels weren't completely tying up her vocal cords.

"Touché." He smiled, and Virginia damn near melted into a puddle on the floor.

Turning away to get a grip back on reality, a reality where this vision of a man was probably doing the horizontal tango with her mother and didn't have any interest in her own skinny self at all, Virginia rambled on, "My mom said something about you having a son?"

"Yeah. He's six and a huge fan of marine life." He followed her into the living room and eyed her as she opened one of the four boxes, examining the brochures with a critical eye due to her need for distraction from how close he was standing. She reached under the table, pulled out a drawer, and extracted a mango-flavored Ring Pop. At Clay's amused look, she shrugged. "It's my favorite candy. Doesn't much matter what people think. Want one?"

"Sure," he replied, surprising her. She offered him a selection and he chose lime. Clay took a brochure from her hand and triggered the same electric reaction all over again, so that Virginia had to mentally scold herself from taking a step back.

Grow up, Ginny. He's not interested and he never will be.

"Does he live with you?" she asked, fumbling for some kind of basic poise, if not at least some fundamental conversational skills.

"He will soon," answered Clay, sliding the Ring Pop into his pocket—not that there was much space, given how snug those jeans were!—doing a neat trifold on the brochure, and putting it aside, then reaching for another. "He's finishing school in Houston, then he's moving in. His only request was that we live on the ocean."

"Maybe he'd be interested in coming to see the dolphins," Virginia suggested, suddenly inspired. "I run the Swim with the Dolphins program. I could get him into the summer volunteer program," she added. "It's a lot of clean-up work, but he'd be around amazing marine animals and dedicated staff."

He folded another brochure and gave her that killer smile.

"That'd be wonderful. Wait until I tell him. There's only a matter of logistics. I leave for work early and don't get home until dark. But I'll figure out something."

"I could take him to work with me and watch him until you get home," Virginia offered.

What's gotten into me? she wondered. *Yeah, he's smokin', but I barely know this man!* She sensed that women flocked to be helpful around this gorgeous, single dad with the rippling muscles.

"Will your mom mind?" he asked, working his way steadily through a tall stack of brochures.

She struggled not to stare at his nimble fingers or wonder what they'd be like doing something far more interesting. "Probably not," replied Virginia. "Let's not play games. She wants you."

Clay looked up from the paper and grinned from ear to ear, utterly unaware of the affect that full-wattage smile had on Virginia. "Yeah. But don't worry. I'm behaving."

She swallowed and almost fanned herself with one of the folded glossies. "That's unusual around my mom. She's gotta be off her game."

"I don't think so. My interests just ...lie elsewhere," Clay murmured.

Was it her imagination or did he lock eyes with her for a long moment when he said that? Totally her imagination. Had to be, as he started for the door.

"When you come over to meet Parker, I'll give you the number for a person who can donate a machine that will do all this folding for you. There are so many other fun things you could be doing ..." With a slow, sexy wink, he vanished into the hallway.

Exhaling a long breath, she collapsed back onto the pillows. *Did that really just happen??*

CHAPTER FIVE

"You're sure you don't mind?" Deanna's voice was slightly slurred over the phone line.

"Of course I do. We were all set for a movie night and you're ditching me for some hot guy in a bar," Virginia replied. "But you do you. You always do."

"Don't be like that ..."

Only drunk Deanna cared much about whether Virginia was offended. Sober Deanna would chalk it up to whining or attention seeking.

"Have fun, Mom. Make sure he uses something. Night." Virginia hung up the phone and stared at it for a second, shaking her head slightly. She had a decent relationship with her mother, but sometimes it felt so ...weird to be the one having to remind her parent to use condoms.

With a sigh, Virginia opened her laptop and signed onto Skype. In an instant, the beloved, geeky face of her best friend, Arty Stone, appeared. Arty stared myopically at the screen and pushed his dark-rimmed glasses up on his nose. Virginia noticed with amusement that Arty's glasses were taped together with adhesive tape and his pocket bore the splotch of an uncapped, blue Sharpie. And he needed a haircut. Arty just never seemed to get around to those life practicalities.

Some things never change, she thought happily. She could always count on Arty to be the stereotypical computer nerd and brilliant scientist he was.

Virginia had met Arty years ago in a chat room for kids with dysfunctional families. His parents had already been legally separated and her parents had been in their pre-divorce stage. She'd been pretty sure her dad was having an affair, and they'd fought all the time. Somehow, she and Arty had made it through the rough years together and had come out stronger in the end, still close friends.

A bit of an insomniac, Arty could always be counted on to respond to her Skype requests day or night.

"What's wrong, Ginny?" he asked, skipping the pleasantries and cutting to the heart of the matter, as was his habit. "You've got that scrunched face thing going again. Mom madness or Dad dick moves this time?"

"The weekend with my dad was surreal," Virginia admitted, setting up beside the laptop with a bunch of brochures. "It's so weird having someone draping herself all over him, and she's, like, my age. Then, I arrived home and made a fool of myself in front of the billionaire next door."

Arty nodded in sarcastic commiseration. "Billionaires will do that to you every time."

"Speaking of doing it ..."

"Your mom wants him?" he guessed immediately. "No surprise."

"Actually, yes, surprise. He's resisting."

Arty's dark eyebrows shot all the way to his hairline. "I think I like him."

"I know I do," Virginia groaned. Thankfully, she and Arty had never had anything but friendly feelings toward one another, and he was actually in a long-term relationship with a great girl, who not only put up with Virginia as his digital 'side piece,' but who saw everything in him that so many other women had overlooked.

Arty smirked. "Hot?"

"As a blue flame."

"Ouch ...how old?"

"He's not old enough for the cougar lady!" Virginia said.

"Did she do the little girl routine? Don't answer. Those eyes say it all."

"Why can't she just be normal?" she sighed. "She got all pissy when she found out I offered to get his son into the Gulf World kids' program. Even though—"

"She volunteered you first," he interrupted, nodding. "Called that one a mile away. So, what's Mr. Blue Flame like?"

"He's donating a machine so I never have to fold these anymore." She held up a brochure.

"Nice. And ... "

"And I did my usual tongue-tied thing. Worse than ever. You'd think that I'd never even kissed a guy!" Virginia wailed.

"Bob behind the bleachers didn't count," he teased, having been her listening ear all through high school drama, as she had been through his. Then he sobered. "Just ...listen, Ginny. This guy may be having a thing with your mother, but he may also have designs on you."

She almost spat out a slug of Mountain Dew, barely avoiding showering her pile of brochures. "Suuuure," Virginia laughed. "Arty, the guy is a god. As in, Mt. Olympus. And, while he may be turning me into Mt. Vesuvius, he's not about to look down from his high home and notice me."

"You always sell yourself short," he remonstrated, holding a hand up as Vanessa called to him off screen, including a faraway hello to Virginia. "One sec."

"Hi, Ness," Virginia called back, folding away industriously and cursing as she gave herself a paper cut.

Arty reappeared a moment later. "Her brother has a flat tire. We've gotta go help him out."

Obviously, he wasn't going to let the love of his life drive around in the middle of the night by herself. Virginia stifled her self-pitying jealousy and waved. "I get it. Be safe."

"Be careful around the guy, Gin," Arty warned again. "You're the one who needs to be safe."

"Go be an amazing boyfriend," she deflected, waving goodbye and cutting the connection.

CHAPTER SIX

The massive bedroom in the Seattle high-rise apartment overlooking Puget Sound was dimly lit by the late-afternoon sun sparkling off the water. Bernie cast loving eyes upon the nubile body of his long-time assistant, Lila Black.

"You're the best, Lila, honey," he sighed. "Sometimes, I think I'd have gone mad if it hadn't been for our afternoons together. Why didn't I marry you?"

"Probably because we'd have made each other miserable," Lila responded with a laugh. "We have a better arrangement, Bernie. You pay me well for my in-the-office and in-the-bedroom assistance," Lila said, patting her pudgy boss' bald head. "You bought me this lovely condo. Your bark is worse than your bite, Bernie. I'm probably the only one who knows you're not the horn dog you make yourself out to be to please those insatiable, bored housewives who hang on your every Dr. Bernie word."

Bernie was about to suggest they have another quick afternoon delight when the phone rang. "Who would be calling here at this time of day?" Bernie groaned.

"There's only one person I can think of," said Lila, handing him the phone.

"What do you want, Deanna?" asked Bernie, picking up the phone.

"That's a pleasant greeting," she noted dryly. "Did I catch you inside your secretary? No. Don't tell me. I really do NOT want to know. I'm just calling because a potential customer is your devoted fan for some reason I don't understand, and you owe me several thousand favors. Put him on your show."

This was how they'd operated ever since their divorce, biting hard at each other, but offering small favors every now and then to offset the pain.

"What's in it for me?" he asked, pulling Lila back down and nuzzling her delicious neck. Her soft sounds of appreciation got him going quickly again, something good for his middle-age ego as much as anything else.

"Publicity. Obviously. My prospective customer is wealthy and insane."

"Done," Bernie agreed, rolling over and wrapping around Lila. "Still hot-to-trot for the bad-boy billionaire next door?"

Deanna's voice dropped several degrees, warning Bernie he'd overstepped the boundaries of their fragile non-relationship. "Go to hell, Bernie. And take the woman in bed with you ... with you."

She hung up the phone.

Lila met Bernie's eyes and they both laughed, although Bernie's laugh was slightly worried. He reached for his phone, pulled up a picture of Deanna's new customer, and showed it to Lila. "Clay Booth. You think my daughter might fall for him?" He'd worried about Virginia ever since her last boyfriend had smashed her heart to smithereens, not that he'd been around when it had happened. Father of the Year wasn't an award he'd ever win.

Lila whistled. "Yes. Yes, I do. Any idea if he's a good guy?"

Feeling slightly jealous at Lila's reaction, Bernie put the phone aside and kissed her hard. "Virginia is so naïve. So damn trusting. No idea where she got that quality." He enjoyed drawing hungry moans from his assistant, trailing his lips down her ample chest and lingering on all the spots he knew she enjoyed.

"I can talk to her," Lila moaned, head falling back. "Warn her. You and Deanna will never get through to her, the way things stand between you. But Virginia and I get along."

"Thanks, babe." He showed his gratitude by draping her legs over his shoulders and diving in.

If you want to continue reading this story, you can get your copy from your favorite vendor by searching for the title:

First Love

A Single Dad Next Door Romance

You can also find the e-book version by typing this link in your computer's browser:

https://www.hotandsteamyromance.com/products/first-love-a-single-dad-next-door-romance

OTHER BOOKS BY THIS AUTHOR

Saving Her Rescuer: A Billionaire & A Virgin Romance

I was just trying to get away from my crazy ex for the weekend when I ended up in a giant pileup on the highway up to Gore Mountain.

https://geni.us/SavingHerRescuer

Sensual Sounds: A Rockstar Ménage

Lust. Lies. Double lives.

The rock and roll industry is full of people who are looking out for themselves and willing to do anything to rise to the top.

https://www.hotandsteamyromance.com/collections/frontpage/products/sensual-sounds-a-rockstar-menage

On the Run: A Secret Baby Romance

Murder. Lies. Fraud. Just another day in the lives of billionaires and women on the run.

https://www.hotandsteamyromance.com/collections/frontpage/products/on-the-run-a-secret-baby-romance

The Dirty Doctor's Touch: A Billionaire Doctor Romance

I am a master. An elitist. I am at the top of my field, and I know what I am doing.

https://www.hotandsteamyromance.com/collections/frontpage/products/the-dirty-doctor-s-touch-a-billionaire-doctor-romance

∼

The Hero She Needs: A Single Daddy Next Door Romance

He's the only man I've ever wanted…

https://www.hotandsteamyromance.com/collections/frontpage/products/the-hero-she-needs-a-single-daddy-next-door-romance

∼

You can find all of my books here:

Hot and Steamy Romance

https://www.hotandsteamyromance.com

∼

Facebook

facebook.com/HotAndSteamyRomance

COPYRIGHT

©Copyright 2020 by Celeste Fall - All rights Reserved

In no way is it legal to reproduce, duplicate, or transmit any part of this document in either electronic means or in printed format. Recording of this publication is strictly prohibited and any storage of this document is not allowed unless with written permission from the publisher. All rights are reserved. Respective authors own all copyrights not held by the publisher.

www.ingramcontent.com/pod-product-compliance
Lightning Source LLC
LaVergne TN
LVHW011731060526
838200LV00051B/3133